THE INCREDIBLE ADVENTURES

OF

DEXTER DUCKWORTH

Part 1: **Goblin Earth**

J A BOWLER

First Published by Springtail 2020

ISBN: 978-1-8380512-0-4

Cover design and illustrations by J A Bowler

Dedicated to those who do not eat ducks.

Contents

Chapter 1

Chance Encounter

Dexter first met the Duckworths the day he fell from the sky into their garden pond. It was a tiny back garden and a tiny pond. Dexter was tiny then too, but he knew what a human was – even one as silly-looking as James in those days when he still had the huge eyes and fat, pudgy cheeks of a three-year-old.

When James reached a stubby hand out towards him, Dexter gave it his best 'stay away' warning, which came out as a pathetic 'peep'. He pecked furiously at the grasping fingers with his little bill, as he was pulled from the water. What a day! First the crow had snatched him away from the safety of his mother's side and then, after a daring escape in mid-air, he had plummeted right into the clutches of a human child.

He was furious. The human made a hideous gurgling sound – it was laughing at him! Dexter wasn't trying to be cute or funny, but the child had its hands cupped round him and was staring at him with those enormous eyes. Dexter realised there was nothing he could do. If he was going to be eaten, at least that would stop the pain that was flaring in his wing. He closed his eyes and waited...

"Don't wowwy, wickle ducky," James had said. "I make oo better," and he took him inside, put him in a big cardboard box and tried to feed him on marshmallows (he ate most of them, himself). It was lucky that James' Dad found Dexter before he came to any serious harm.

The duckling watched as they tapped their fingers on Dad's phone screen to look up, 'What do baby mallards eat?' on the Internet. It seems they don't normally eat marshmallows. Who knew?

Dexter was much happier with the chopped vegetables suggested by the wildlife site, and it seemed like a safe place to stay till his wing got better. Which eventually it did, but Dexter never left.

They had taken him down to the river when he was better, to try to get him to live with the other ducks again, but it was a disaster. His mother and brothers and sisters had long since moved on and the other ducks were not very pleased to see him back.

When Dexter went home the next day, James' Dad opened the door to find him standing on the front step looking cross. He gave them the whole story and told them not to do it again. Of course, it just sounded like a lot of angry peeps to them — but after staring at him stupidly for a few seconds, they let him back in.

"Well, James, we'd better give him a name then, if he's going to stay," Dad said. "Let's see... Ducky... erm no, that's too obvious... Drake... hmm... I think that one may be a bit boring. What about Dexter? After Great-Uncle Dexter Duckworth?" And then he laughed a lot. He obviously thought it was very funny to have a duck in the Duckworth family.

"What do you think of that, Dexter?" Dad said, talking to the duck as though he could answer. Dexter peeped and waggled off through the back door, out to the garden and into the pond where he eyed the two humans for a moment before tipping upside down in the water and sticking his tail in the air.

James must have been impressed because he spent the evening pretending to be a duckling, running around the house, and sticking his own 'tail' up in the air.

Chapter 2

Gogzi

I know not everyone has a duck in the family, but people have dogs and cats and gerbils and goldfish and some people even have snakes and spiders. By the time James was at school, Dexter had become used to being a normal part of the Duckworth family life. He was free to wander about the little back garden and had his own 'duck-flap' in the front door so that he could come in if he wanted. He was careful to never make any mess in the house.

When James came home from school, Dexter would be sitting on the sofa in the lounge watching old black and white movies on the telly. Maybe that's odd behaviour for a duck but James never questioned it. After all you don't question things when you've never known any different.

One day, James arrived home and went into the lounge to check on his friend, but Dexter wasn't there. It was a little odd, but James didn't panic. Dexter was free to come and go as he liked. He told his dad that he'd just have a look round the house and down by the shops.

"Perhaps he's having a swim in the canal," Dad suggested. James was doubtful about this, but he went to look anyway. Scruffy, urban ducks lined the banks of the canal. They no longer looked like wild mallards, through years of mixing with white domestic ducks and other darker species. People had thrown bread for them and the whole place was a mess. Expecting food, they gave low quacks as James approached, but he couldn't see Dexter's shiny purple and green plumage anywhere among them.

Suddenly, James was startled as a small, dark creature jumped out in front of him, brandishing a feather.

"Hahah!" the creature cried, as though it had just caught James out. "Me is Gogzi!" It sounded like a cross between a cough and a sneeze. James didn't know how to respond.

His eyes widened at the sight before him. The creature had a human-like form but was shorter and a lot skinnier. Large, bright eyes shone out of its greenish face, and it smiled to reveal two rows of tiny, sharp teeth. It had two outsized, pointed ears which poked out from the wiry reddish-brown hair that sprouted punkishly from the creature's head. This was then tied in a loose plait that hung down its back.

James felt that it was a female whatever-it-was. She was wearing a rough skirt and a studded leather vest. Her skinny arms and legs were completely bare but on her feet she wore a pair of spiky boots. She had sharp nails, like talons, and in her hand she brandished a long, wooden stick which ended in a dangerous-looking point. Before James could answer her, the little figure waved the stick at him and shouted again.

"Gogzi is best goblin chief!" she cried. "Me is take duck friend! Hahah!" She sounded triumphant, as though she had won some kind of contest.

"What?" James replied, his mind taking time to register the strange creature and its threatening message. He stared at the little goblin who waved the feather under his nose. It was just like one of Dexter's. It *was* one of Dexter's! The goblin flicked the feather from finger to finger but when James grabbed at it, it fizzled and burned away in a puff of greasy smoke. Gogzi disappeared.

James stared at the spot where the goblin had been, straining to find where she had gone, but when he stepped forward, he bumped into something he couldn't see.

"An invisible wall!" James thought, immediately. He knew what it was. Not everybody would have, but James' Dad had read him lots of stories when he was little. They had taught him about goblins and elves and tree-creatures and water-sprites. He had learned about strange other worlds and magic portals. He loved that stuff. They had also taught him that you don't abandon your friends. Gogzi's glee at kidnapping Dexter had made James cross, which is probably why he didn't do the sensible thing and go home to tell his father.

Chapter 3

Captured

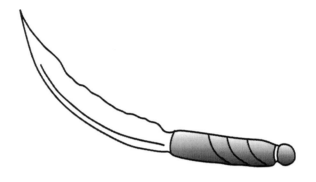

James could feel the smooth, solid surface of the invisible barrier. He crept along the wall, both hands pressed against it, searching for a gap. Suddenly his right hand slipped forward and disappeared. James stared for a moment. It was bizarre and unpleasant to see his arm ending at the elbow and then just the background of the canal bridge behind. He glanced around to check if anyone was watching but his only companions were the scruffy ducks and a few Canada geese.

James pulled his hand back sharply, fearful of what might be on the other side of the barrier. When he reached forward again, he could clearly make out the edge of what must have been a doorway through the wall. Summoning up his courage and thinking of his friend, he stepped through. He could only have been there a second when he was roughly grabbed by several pairs of bony hands.

He tried to cry out and move back toward the door, but he was being held too tightly. One of his captors threw a dirty sack over James' head and in spite of his frantic wriggling to escape, he was dragged across an unfamiliar landscape and into a tunnel. He could hear Dexter in the distance, quacking, and the peculiar noises of goblin activity getting louder and louder.

"Where are you taking me?" he cried.

"Shut mouth, human prisoner!" the goblins replied in their harsh voices. He was pushed through the jagged, dark tunnels and thrown roughly into a cave-like room.

"Dexter!" he cried, hearing the duck quacking miserably nearby. He could not see that his friend had his wings bound with a dirty rag. "Are you alright? What's going on?"

The goblins hissed at him spraying spittle. He struggled and shook his head to try to throw off the sack, but they bundled him onto the floor and tied his hands to the rusty iron bracket that was embedded in the cave wall.

"They're going to keep us here," quacked Dexter, when the goblins had gone, "and put a goblin boy in your place back home!"

James was astonished to be able to understand Dexter's words, even though he struggled to know what he was talking about.

"You can speak!" he whispered back.

"I could always speak," Dexter replied haughtily. "You just didn't know how to listen. It must be this place – it's not our world. It's different. We can talk to each other here."

"How long will they keep us?" queried James. Dexter shrugged his wings.

"It depends on when they want to eat you!" he quacked.

Inside his sack blindfold, James turned pale. He really didn't like that idea.

"That's disgusting!" he replied. "They eat humans?"

"Humans eat ducks," Dexter retorted huffily. "Is that not disgusting?"

James had to concede. He personally had never eaten a duck, but he knew that Dexter had a point. Humans ate a lot of animals. Was it so different?

He intended to escape before that happened, though. He started pulling at the tough rope that attached him to the wall bracket. It wouldn't budge. He had to find something to cut it. James leaned forward and dipped his head, pushing the sack down and managing to clasp the end of it between his knees. As he sat up, the sack was pulled off and he could look around himself for the first time.

The room was dimly-lit with flickering, primitive lamps jutting from the rocky walls. He could see Dexter at his side, looking ruffled but unharmed. Just as he was peering about for some way of getting free, his attention was taken by a horrendous noise like the release of air from a giant balloon; a huge animal barged into the cave and skidded to a halt in front of him.

James shrank back against the wall at the sight of the beast. It was the size of a rhino, with the same thick, wrinkled skin, but instead of a single horn, it had two enormous tusks. From the top of its head between its small, flicking ears, and down the middle of its back, grew a long, bristly mane. It had broad, three-toed feet and small piggy eyes which were blinking in the dim light.

James could feel his heart pounding in alarm, but the creature stood still. She was making a low rumbling noise and filling the air with the stench of rotting cabbage. Beneath her, James could just see another little creature – a smaller version of the beast – its baby. The 'calf' (or perhaps it was a 'piglet') was making gentle grunting noises and scrabbling about under the heaving tummy of its mother. It was cute in an ugly sort of way.

"She's the goblins' animal," Dexter informed James. "She's a fartlebeast. Don't ask. I have no idea what they do with her! She seems tame, but try not to do anything to upset her."

James was just wondering what kinds of things would upset a fartlebeast, when he heard the cackle of goblin laughter. One of them followed the animal into the room and held out a pot of foul-smelling goo. He shoved it forwards under James' nose, showing it to him and sniggering.

"Is best stick stuff ever!" boasted the goblin.

James stared glumly at the disgusting mixture and wrinkled his nose.

"Why are you telling me about your horrible glue?" he shouted angrily. The goblin snickered and leaned in closer to James till they were almost touching noses. James turned his head away.

"We is use it stick-stick human prisoner," he answered cheekily, He scooped out a glob of the stuff and waved his dripping hand at the walls with a flourish, as though James should be proud to be the goblins' next piece of artwork hanging there.

The goblin winked rudely at James and gave the fartlebeast a smug smack of satisfaction on her rump. Unfortunately for him, this was one of those things that *would* upset a fartlebeast. Her piggy eyes opened wide with surprise and she gave a roar of disapproval. She stomped the ground and rotated surprisingly quickly to express her annoyance at the insult. But the glue had lived up to its reputation for being the best; the goblin's hand was stuck fast to her hindquarters and as she turned, he was whipped round like a scrawny, green tail.

This seemed to upset her even more and she shot off down the tunnel, farting loudly, followed by her baby and the hapless goblin who was dragged along still sticking to her behind. For a moment, James and Dexter were alone and James could see that in the chaos, the unfortunate goblin had dropped something on the cave floor.

"Quick!" quacked Dexter. "It's time to start making our escape."

Not wasting a moment, Dexter chewed on the ropes that bound James' hands, until he could wriggle free. James scrambled across the dirty floor and grabbed the object. It was a goblin weapon – a knife with a small, curved blade. It was sharp and deadly and just the thing he needed to cut the grubby cloth that the goblins had used to bind Dexter. When the duck was free, James tucked the blade in his trouser belt, and ran out into the tunnels.

Chapter 4

Escape

Escape was easier said than done, however. Even if James had not been blindfolded on his journey in, he wouldn't have known which way to go. All the tunnels looked the same and there were many forks and branches. There was no sign of light that might indicate a way out. James' only thought was that he needed to run away from the sounds of the goblins who were laughing and seemed to be singing or chanting something in their strange, guttural language.

Dexter appeared to have a better idea of direction and flew ahead, stopping now and then to let the slow human catch up on foot. As he ran, James tried not to look too closely at the grisly items that were sticking to the walls. The remains of past prisoners. Hopefully he would avoid their fate, now!

In the distance, they could hear the sound of goblins cheering. It was like they were having a party. Maybe it was a feast in which he was supposed to be the main course! The horrible thought spurred James on.

"This way!" quacked Dexter, landing in front and pointing the way with his wing. James hesitated. It looked like Dexter was turning down a darker tunnel that was leading them back towards the festivities.

"Are you sure?" James asked.

Dexter squinted at him for a moment as though James was incredibly stupid. He fluffed his feathers and gave a brief waggle of annoyance.

"Yes, of course!" he replied. "You know that ducks have a built-in navigation system don't you? It's like our own little compass in our head."

James felt it was the sort of thing he should know. He made a mental note to learn a lot more about it when he finally got home. If he ever got home!

"OK, Let's go." he replied. At that point, James noticed that it had grown unusually quiet – it was not a good sign.

"Fly!" he whispered urgently and they both plunged into the dark tunnel. Beneath his feet, James could feel that the floor was sloping upwards, but there was no light to see by. He followed the flapping sound of Dexter's wings and then, just as he was beginning to totally lose confidence that they had gone the right way, he could just see Dexter's silhouette against the distant light of the exit. His heart skipped a beat. They were nearly there!

Suddenly a goblin stepped in front of James and they both tumbled to the ground. James recognised her. It was Gogzi! Immediately, Dexter leaped on top of the goblin, pecking her and flapping his wings in her face but Gogzi still had James tightly held in her grasp. For a small creature, she had amazing strength.

"Ow! Stop it, horrid duck friend!" Gogzi, cried, trying to push away Dexter's wings with one hand while hanging on to James with the other. The distraction gave James the chance to grab the goblin blade he had tucked into his belt. He managed to pull it out and raise it above his head, threatening to bring it down on Gogzi who was now on her back in the dirt. James wasn't sure if he really would have been able to use the blade, but as Gogzi caught sight of it, the little goblin froze and stared at the weapon with wide, frightened eyes. She dropped both scrawny hands to her sides and closed her eyes as if waiting for the fatal blow.

James did not have long to make a decision. Hearing the raucous shouting of the goblins growing louder, he scrambled to his feet, with Gogzi still waiting, eyes shut, and pulled Dexter away. Worried their fight would draw attention and with Dexter still quacking in fury, he plunged towards the exit and stumbled out into the light.

As he ran, with Dexter flying overhead, James noticed that all around was a strange land. He had never seen anything like it before. On every side, they were surrounded by flat, boggy ground dotted with spiky marsh plants. A few leafless trees grew, their branches reaching upwards like desperate fingers in the fading light.

James could hear the chirping and croaking call and response of hidden animals but he had no idea what they were. By his feet there was the occasional 'plop' where damp, frog-like things jumped out of his path as he ran.

His feet were getting soaked and he was concerned that he would sink into the sticky mud.

"Which way do we go?" James called up to his pet.

Chapter 5

Imposter

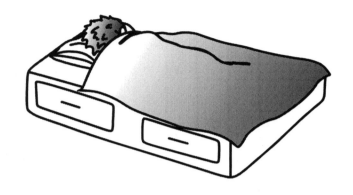

Flapping overhead, Dexter had a good view of the countryside. The goblins had not bothered to blindfold the duck when they had captured him. For a while he did not answer, scanning the terrain for something familiar that would tell him where the barrier to their world was. He could see features he had passed before.

At once there was the recognisable skeleton of an old, half collapsed stone tower by a lake. The surface of the lake was smooth and still, like a vast black mirror.

"This way!" he called, turning quickly and diving down towards a brighter patch of sky.

By now, James could hear the angry shouts of the goblins and the splashing of their feet close behind. Frightened that they would catch up and take him and Dexter back to their cave, he redoubled his efforts, sprinting as fast as he could.

As the two of them reached the shimmering doorway to their own world, numerous bony little hands grabbed for James, clutching at his clothes and scratching his arms with their sharp nails, but this time they could not hold on.

James dived towards the portal just as he saw Dexter make it through overhead.

On their side, the sun was just rising. Intense rays shone straight at the goblins who shrieked and covered their eyes and were driven back to their own world. Without looking back, James raced for home. His dad's car was still on the drive.

"Why isn't he out looking for me?" James asked.

"You forget," replied Dexter, "he doesn't know you're missing because there's a goblin changeling in your place. Dad will be under its spell by now and will think it's you and that there's nothing wrong. Meanwhile the goblin boy will be eating your food and getting you into trouble at school!"

Amazingly, James could still understand Dexter's words. Something in Goblin Earth must have triggered his ability to hear what the duck was saying, even when they were back in the human world. He looked horrified at Dexter's analysis. What kinds of things would the goblin changeling have been doing while James was away? He tried the front door but it was locked, of course, and James did not have a key. Dexter was about to use the duck-flap when James put out a hand to stop him.

"Wait!" he said. "We don't know that it's safe." He made his way down the side of the house and into the garden. On the back wall, there was a drainpipe that led down from the gutter on the roof and past his bedroom to the ground. While Dexter went straight for the pond, James used the pipe to climb up to his window and peer in. The goblin changeling was asleep in his bed.

It was lying facing away from the window but it had dark, scruffy hair and was wearing James' pyjamas. Suddenly it turned towards them. It looked just like James!

The goblin opened its eyes and stared straight at him. James nearly let go of the drainpipe in shock. The imposter smiled and James could see its pointy teeth. How could his father not have noticed those?

There was a gap where the window was partly open. Pulling it wider, James climbed in and rolled onto the floor. Immediately, the goblin boy jumped out of bed and threw himself at James.

"Hah! Bad human boy! Is not be here! Is home for goblin boy. Boy dad is goblin dad, now!"

The thought of the goblin boy taking his place and having his dad as its own made James feel sick. He was struggling to hold it off as it tried to push James towards the open window. Now that James could see him up close, he really did not look as much like him as he had first thought. The goblin was much shorter, for a start, and he had pitch black irises, unlike James' hazel eyes. If people were fooled, Dexter was right – it had to be because the goblins could cast some sort of spell.

The goblin boy fought furiously. James could feel sharp nails cutting into him. As he tried to push him off, the goblin sunk his teeth into James' shoulder and James gave a yelp of pain. He called out loudly for his father, but there was no response.

"Stupid human boy!" shouted the goblin. "Boy dad is not come. Is take goblin sleep-sleep drink. Is not wake for big time."

So that was it! The goblin had used some sort of potion on his dad to keep him asleep or drugged so that he didn't notice there was something different about his son.

James was being cut and bruised by the ferocious attack of his imposter and was beaten back to the window. Looking out, he could see Dexter had flown up to the ledge and was quacking at him.

"James, this is no use! Come down. We need to think about what to do."

James had no choice. He climbed back out of the window and down the drainpipe. Looking up, he saw the goblin child leaning out. It licked its lips and laughed.

"Go, tasty human boy!" it sniggered. "Is make nice meal if come back!"

But James could not quite bring himself to leave yet. He felt awful and he wanted desperately to speak to his father. Followed by Dexter, he went back round to the front of the house and tried to look in through the lounge window.

The curtains were drawn, but there was a small crack where he could just about see in. It was dingy inside. His heart gave a skip as he made out the shape of his father, seated in his favourite armchair. Hope led quickly to disappointment, though. His dad was slumped awkwardly, clearly asleep. When James rapped on the window, he turned his head slowly and his eyelids fluttered, but that was all.

Chapter 6

Naklog

James and Dexter needed a plan and they needed to leave the garden for somewhere safe from the goblin changeling. Somehow, they had to get rid of him and get Dad back to reality. Dexter suggested they should go back to the canal-side where James had found the portal. If it was still there, maybe they would come up with an idea to get the goblin boy to go back.

James sat on the bench staring gloomily at the murky water, while Dexter paddled in amongst the scruffy town ducks. Although they were annoyed at his presence, they did nothing but glower at him crossly and make soft quacks of disapproval, aware that the human was close by. The Canada geese ignored Dexter completely, merely keeping a watchful eye in case James had brought bread.

He had not been able to find the invisible barrier, nor the doorway to the goblin realm. He had thought that if he could capture the changeling, he could bring him here and push him through. But there was no sign of it and even if there had been, they would need to close the portal afterwards, and James had no idea how to do that.

"Who would know about this stuff?" he asked Dexter.

Dexter shrugged his wings.

"Me is know who," came a familiar harsh voice from behind.

James turned. Not Gogzi, again! She was wearing a hooded cloak that covered her face, but there was no mistaking that voice.

James jumped up and felt for his goblin knife. Dexter clambered out of the canal and ran towards Gogzi, quacking angrily.

"No! Keep off, horrid bird!" shouted Gogzi. "Me is help. Me is help! Me is know what to do."

James paused, his hand halfway to the knife. What was the little goblin saying? Was this a trick?

"What do you mean?" James said, cautiously. "How can you help? Why would you? You just want to take me back so I can be dinner!"

"No, please," said Gogzi. Boy is tasty dinner, is true. But me is not eat. Is not take back, now. Boy is not kill Gogzi so me is help boy."

James thought about this for a moment. Was Gogzi saying what he thought she was saying? He had spared Gogzi's life and now the goblin was going to help him?

"What do you think, Dexter?" James asked.

"I don't think we have much choice," said Dexter. "But I wouldn't trust her further than I could throw her. And have you ever seen ducks throw? We're rubbish at it."

James sighed and said, 'OK, how can you help? Careful, though. I'm watching you! Don't try anything funny, or else!" James wasn't sure what the 'else' would be, but it sounded like he meant it.

"Me is know who is help," Gogzi repeated. "Naklog is old goblin. Is live long time human world. We is make big walk now. See Naklog. Make talk-talk."

James distilled this information. He glanced at Dexter, who appeared to be preening his feathers and not really listening. Did they really have any other option?

"OK," James replied. "We'll visit this Nag... Nak... this old goblin..."

"Naklog," Gogzi interjected.

"Yes," James went on. "But no tricks. I've still got this." He put his hand on his knife.

Gogzi nodded and led the way down the canal tow path. Dexter followed on the water.

James had no idea where they were going nor how far. Whenever he asked Gogzi, the goblin replied by shaking her head and saying, "We is make big walk."

"Yes, but how big is big?" James muttered to himself. He had had no sleep last night, and not having eaten for hours was giving him sharp pangs of hunger. He envied Dexter, who could just drift on the canal, hardly having to move his feet as paddles, now and then dipping his head under and nibbling at the weed if he felt hungry. Gogzi, herself, seemed full of energy and set a fast pace that he struggled to keep up with.

It was early evening by the time Gogzi put out her bony, little hand in a gesture to stop. They had been walking for an entire day with only the occasional break so that James could shake the pebbles out of his shoes.

"Is here!" Gogzi announced, making them stop unexpectedly.

James looked around. There was nothing to see except the canal and a small brick building, not much bigger than a garden shed.

"This?" he asked, pointing at the building.

"We is see," Gogzi said.

She knocked on the door of the hut. It was a complicated rhythm that seemed to go on for ages. Just as

45

James began to suspect that Gogzi was making fun of them, the door creaked open a little and he could just see the glint of a shiny black eye as the owner peeped out.

"Naklog!" Gogzi shouted. "Is Gogzi! Open. We is need help."

"Gogzi... is that you?" the occupant asked, pulling the door open a little more, to reveal an ancient, wrinkled face blinking in the sunlight. It was difficult to tell if it was male or female, human or goblin. What might have been the tell-tale greenish skin was so covered in dirt and grime it could have been any hue beneath.

The old creature glanced suspiciously at James and then stared at Dexter from under a straggly fringe of grey hair. James could see that it was wearing human clothes – a kind of long, baggy shirt, or a dress. He was not sure which. It may once have had some kind of floral design but that was now so faded and mixed with stains of various sorts that they could not be certain.

"What are you bringing me, Gogzi? Whatever it is, I'm not interested. Go away and leave me alone. I'm just a poor old woman trying to live a quiet life!" The way she spoke was almost human but it had a grating edge that gave away her other-world origins. James could see Dexter shudder slightly. The old hag began to shut the door.

Gogzi laughed and stepped in to stop her from closing it.

"Naklog is not woman! Naklog is goblin! Me is know Naklog from long time. Naklog is not be poor. Naklog is

not be quiet. Open. We is come in."
Gogzi pushed the door, forcing the 'old
woman' back into her dark hut.
Slightly reluctantly, James and
Dexter followed.

The inside of the hut seemed to
contain more stuff than was possible
for its size. In the pale light from its
one grimy window, James could see
the lumpy shape of what could have
been the goblin's bed. He recognised
some items among the jumble of
objects stacked on rickety wooden
shelves. There were obviously pots for
cooking and what looked like the dried
husks of old vegetables. James
thought he could see a couple of
wheels and bits of old bicycles –
probably salvaged from the canal.
Other things were less obvious and
James was not keen to find out what

they were. The whole place had a damp, muddy smell. It was not pleasant.

"What do you want, Gogzi?" the goblin asked, sounding much less like a helpless old woman now. "Why have you brought me these?" She was still eyeing Dexter, who had jumped up on to a chunky wooden table, and she hardly glanced at James. Gogzi paused. She seemed to be weighing up what to say. She looked from James to Dexter to Naklog and then back to James.

"Me is want help human boy, James... and horrid duck friend," she said, eventually. "Is not want goblin boy take this human place. This human dad. Goblin boy is go back. Not return. Naklog is know how."

Naklog snarled and showed her teeth. Though she was obviously ancient, she still had two perfect rows and they looked as sharp as ever.

"Gogzi. You are a stupid goblin! And now a traitor!" Naklog spat. "Take these things out of my home at once! What makes you think I would do anything to help those?" She meant James and Dexter! She started to push the little goblin towards the door but Gogzi had no intention of leaving. She gave Naklog a shove and the old goblin sat suddenly on her bed, a look of surprise and outrage on her face. She started up again as if to attack, but Gogzi pushed her back with both hands.

"Naklog is help," Gogzi said, all warmth gone from her voice. "Me is know Naklog secret. Naklog is not like if me is tell all other goblins what me is know. Naklog is give help – then me is not tell."

If goblins could go pale, this might have been visible. As it was, Gogzi's words seemed to stop the old crone in mid protest and she slumped back down as though defeated.

James and Dexter gave each other a puzzled look that said neither of them were sure what was going on. The old goblin hissed, but the fight seemed to have gone out of her.

"If I help this time, Gogzi, then you go away and never come here again?" It wasn't clear whether she was threatening or begging, but Gogzi nodded.

"Me is go back. Is take goblin boy."

She glowered at him.

"You realise what you are saying? You will not be able to…"

Gogzi interrupted her before she could finish.

"Is plan," she said, briefly, nodding at Naklog and raising one finger. "Me is do this."

Naklog pushed some things aside and waved at James to sit, which he did reluctantly, trying to avoid dark or sticky patches.

Dexter seemed happy on the table and began preening his feathers. All the time the old goblin kept him in her sights and made James feel very uneasy.

Gogzi squeezed herself in between some pots on the rickety shelf. She had to bend over slightly to avoid hitting her head on the ceiling. The old goblin pointed to her and said,

"You come to me, Gogzi, because you think you know my story. I trusted you once and now you use this against me. But you are young. I am older than even you know and my secrets are older than you can imagine. I remember the time before the Great Divide. The time when goblins roamed freely on this Earth. The time before the humans and their machines. This was all goblin land. Now it is over-run with your species and goblins are kept in that dark land behind the wall!"

She scowled at James before continuing.

"The only way we could come here was by hiding or by trickery. By taking the place of a human. By becoming a changeling." She spat the word out with surprising venom, as though she hated the very idea.

Gogzi looked at the ground. She seemed embarrassed or sad.

"Nuin is be safe, Naklog," she said. "Is make good goblin cakes. Is have three fartlebeast!"

James was confused. He could just about understand some of the words but had no idea what either of them was talking about.

Naklog looked at Gogzi and raised her eyebrows before staring out of the grimy window.

"Hah! So now you bring me this news of my daughter. She's alive and well, you tell me!" She said it with a growl which made it hard to know if it meant good news or bad. "But she knows nothing of me! I have given up everything. No goblin daughter. No goblin grandchildren. You know this, but you come here and taunt me with your requests."

Gogzi looked at James and then at Dexter and back again.

"Me is explain," she said. "Nuin is Naklog girl baby. Goblin baby. Long time before, Goblin King is say Nuin must go human world. Take place of tasty human baby. Naklog is not want. Naklog is steal key. Is rescue human baby from Goblin King. Is swap back for own child, Nuin. Is hide Nuin in Gogzi village when me is small. Naklog is give Nuin to Gogzi Mum. Is pay big gold. Nuin is like Gogzi sister. We is keep safe. We is never tell secret."

"Until now!" snarled Naklog, shooting Gogzi a terrible look.

"You is help human and duck-friend," Gogzi retorted. "Then secret is safe forever."

The old goblin seemed to be thinking about this. She bustled around the hut as though looking for something. Eventually she tipped out the contents of a ceramic pot and held up a small item. It looked like it was made out of yellow metal. She showed it to James. It was in the shape of a twisted tree branch – intricate and clearly made by someone with a lot of skill. At one end was a small loop that indicated that it had probably hung on a chain.

"Goblin gold!" Naklog said, proudly. "This medallion was part of our key. Once there were two sides. Two trees intertwined. One represented the human side of the barrier and the other the goblin realm. The king was the only one allowed to open the barrier and all the human babies were his. All he needed to do, was to pull the two sides apart and the doorway to your world would open. When he put them back together, it would close. I did a terrible thing when I stole the key. I opened the door to your world so that I could bring my child home and return the human baby that was stolen. It was forbidden for goblins to leave the realm without permission. When I did that, I sealed my fate. The King found out what I had done and put a price on my head. I knew it was not safe for Nuin if I was in the goblin realm. They would find me and kill me and they would take her back. So I came to your side and I hid. I should have closed the medallion and sealed off the goblin world forever. But I couldn't bear the thought of never going back. Of never being reunited with my Nuin. So I separated the two parts of the key and I threw away the other part."

"But that means the door is open," James said at last. Can't we just take the goblin boy back through it? We just need your help to find the way."

At this point Dexter interrupted. He shook his head at James and said, "That wouldn't work, James. While the door is open, the goblins will come back. You'll never know when. You'll never be able to sleep. And next time, neither of us might be so lucky. The goblins would be having a roast human dinner – with duck as a side-dish."

James shuddered. He knew what Dexter was saying. They needed to take the changeling back and close the door forever. It was time to stop the goblins entering the human world.

"Where did you put the other half?" he asked Naklog, who was staring intently at Dexter.

"You cannot get it," she said, simply. Gogzi frowned.

"Me is tell truth, Naklog. You is help or secret is no more."

"I said *you* cannot get it," she restated, pointing at James. "But *he* can!"

She stuck out a bony finger at Dexter, directing a sharp talon straight at his newly-preened chest feathers.

"What?" he quacked, backing off a little. "Why me?"

"You are a duck," she replied. "But not any old duck are you? These ducks – all they think about is food and squabbling. They're stupid ducks. I've tried talking to them. They can do duck things but they can't understand. But you can, can't you? I knew it as soon as I saw you."

James was as confused as ever.

"What do you mean?" he asked. "How can Dexter being a duck help? He's a great duck and a good friend. He helped me out a lot in the last two days, but he mainly swims, eats weeds and watches telly." James looked at Dexter and shrugged and Dexter nodded in agreement.

The old goblin sighed and rolled her eyes.

"I will show you," she said. "Come!"

James rose stiffly from his seat. His feet hurt. He wondered if this was what it was like when you got old. He followed the ancient goblin, with Dexter and Gogzi, out of the hut to the side of the canal.

"There!" she said, pointing at the opaque, brown water of the canal. Then she shrugged. "Somewhere, there. The other half. I threw it in a long time ago."

Then James understood. She meant the other half of the medallion was at the bottom of the canal, probably buried deep in the soft mud below. Or perhaps it had drifted down the canal with each opening and closing of the lock gates to let the water and the boats through. If so, they hadn't much chance of finding it. To get it back, someone, or more precisely, some duck would have to dive down and search for it. If they had a lot of diving gear, perhaps a human could do it, but Dexter was born for this. He quacked an interruption.

"Really?" he asked. "You really want me to dive down there?" He nodded at the canal with his duckbill.

James was a bit surprised.

"I thought that's what you ducks do..." he started. Dexter waggled huffily.

"I dip in the surface, "he replied. "Have you any idea what kinds of things are at the bottom of a canal? No sensible duck ever goes down there. It's a death-trap! If it's not sharp sticking out things — twisted old bike frames and shopping trolleys — it's long strands of old rope and plastic caught on the rubbish, waiting to snare any creature that is unfortunate enough to get itself tangled in it."

They stood in silence all looking at each other. James needed that key but could he ask Dexter to do something he so obviously did not wish to? Eventually, Naklog made a snort of derision and went inside her hut, leaving the three others standing by the side of the canal. It was Gogzi who spoke first. Her voice was unusually quiet.

"Duck friend is do this, no? After, is splash big time in little round water. Look at magic telly pictures. Human boy, James, is not be tasty goblin eating."

Dexter knew that she was right. He was going to do this for James who had, after all, come to rescue him.

"Wait here!" he quacked, and without another word, jumped into the water with a splash, gave a wiggle of his tail and ducked under. James and Gogzi stared after him.

It seemed like ages, but it was probably only a few seconds later, that Dexter emerged with something in his beak and plopped it on the side of the canal. James' pulse quickened but when he looked, it was only an old bottle top. Dexter tried again. And again. Soon there was a pile of small twisted pieces of metal and a lot of mud on the bank, but nothing that resembled the second half of the key. Dexter looked exhausted.

"Stop!" James cried. "This is pointless! We're never going to find something as small as that after all this time."

From inside the hut came the sound of goblin laughter which quickly became a fit of coughing and then Naklog emerged into the sunlight again.

"You've found much treasure, I see!" she cackled. She rooted through the debris and raised a misshapen lump of metal into the air. "Ah! My old salt spoon! I wondered where that had gone!"

Dexter flopped on to the side of the canal and gave her his best duck scowl. Naklog looked at them all for a moment and then she pulled out the medallion. She had tied it to a greyish string which looked unpleasantly like it was made of her own goblin hair. She was holding it by this when something remarkable began to happen.

At first, the medallion swung to and fro like a small pendulum, but gradually it began to linger a little more at one side than the other, until it was distinctly pulling in a direction towards the canal.

"Key is want be together!" Gogzi cried. "Is show where."

"Yes," said Naklog. "The two halves are attracted to each other. You cannot tell unless you do it like this."

"You knew this and yet you let Dexter waste all that time and energy looking!" James was outraged. Naklog sniggered.

"I wanted to see what he would come up with," she replied. "There's lots of good stuff down there." If Dexter could have pulled a face of disgust, he would have. "Also, to see if the key could be found. It was most amusing to watch."

Dexter had listened enough. As she was dangling the key from its string of hair, he grabbed it in his bill and plunged once more into the murky water. By now the light was nearly gone from the sky. The others could only just see him when he bobbed back up a few metres along, the medallion still held in his bill; it was pointing down the canal. He disappeared under again. And then nothing.

James began to panic. Dexter had said it was dangerous down there. He could have got caught up on something. Ducks can swim but they can't survive underwater forever. Then Gogzi shouted, "Look!" and pointed into the distance. In the dim light, they could just see Dexter emerging from the canal some considerable distance away. He jumped on to the side and gave a shake, sending droplets of water flying off his feathers. Triumphantly he held up his bill, both parts of the medallion now joined at the end of the string.

Chapter 7

Cheese on Toast

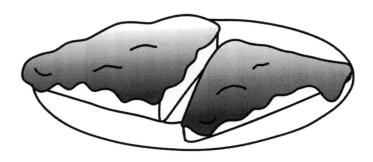

Naklog hissed. James could not tell if it was a hiss of triumph or annoyance, but he wasn't waiting to find out. He ran to Dexter and lifted him off the ground. He was wet and he smelled of stinky mud but James didn't care.

"That's a little undignified, but alright," Dexter said, paddling his feet in the air as James hugged him. "You're welcome."

The pair rejoined Gogzi and Naklog who were engaged in a conversation along the canal-side.

"You is not come too?" Gogzi asked. "You is see Nuin, perhaps?"

Naklog scowled at her and spat out the words, "You know I cannot return, Gogzi! Not while the Goblin King sits on the throne. And now you will finish things forever. Go and leave me!"

She pushed the little goblin away and retired to her hut, shutting the door firmly.

All three of them stared after her. They could still see her looking at them through the window. Dexter gave her a little quack and a wave of his wing and she ducked down in annoyance. Then he turned to the others.

"What now?" he asked. "Please say I don't have to do any more diving into mud."

"Now we is get goblin boy," Gogzi replied. "Save James Dad. Me is have plan."

"Another plan," Dexter quacked dismissively, but he turned to James and they both knew they still needed Gogzi's help.

"First, I is pay visit to goblin boy," she went on. "We is eat together."

James' stomach rumbled at the thought of food. How long since he had eaten? Nearly two days? Gogzi looked at him and gave a goblin snicker of laughter.

"Then me is also bring human food," she said. "But first, me is tell Best Plan."

After Gogzi had explained it from start to finish, James wasn't sure if it was the *best* plan but hunger was making him light-headed. He thought of the big block of cheese in the fridge. He thought of his comfortable bed. He thought of his dad, who was kept asleep by goblin potions, and he wanted to get back to normality as soon as possible.

When James climbed back up the drainpipe, he could see, with a flush of anger, that his look-alike was still in his room. Following Gogzi's plan, James gave the nod down to her and she hurried round to the front door.

"Now!" she said to Dexter who went in through the duck-flap as quietly as he could so as not to alert the goblin inside. Dexter could not open the door himself, but the key was lying in a dish on a small table in the hall. He grabbed this in his bill and jumped back out through the flap. By this time, James had joined them at the front of the house.

Gogzi passed the key to him and he turned it in the lock, trying his best to avoid the clicking sound that would give them away. He desperately wanted to rush in and try to wake his father, but he knew that they needed to stick to the plan.

With the door just ajar, James and Dexter watched as Gogzi went in alone. They were to guard the house and stop the changeling if he tried to leave, but keep the door open so that they could get in when the time was right. Once inside, Gogzi used all her goblin skill not to make any noise. She knew that the changeling would have the brilliant hearing of a goblin, and she had to complete the task before it became aware of her presence.

Gogzi crept over to James' dad. He looked fast asleep, but uncomfortable in his work clothes which were all dishevelled and he had several days of beard stubble showing. Gogzi reached over and prised open one of his eyelids. James' dad gave a snort and shifted in his chair, but he did not wake up. The potion was too strong and Gogzi could smell it nearby. She followed the scent trail to a cup on the kitchen table. The goblin must have slipped it into Dad's coffee. Now she just needed to find the rest of it.

Gogzi peered around the kitchen. There were signs that the

goblin boy had raided all the food stores. Empty packets were scattered on the surfaces and there were several open tins, their contents mostly eaten; the remains were already sprouting green mould, suggesting that more time had passed here on the human side of the barrier than in Goblin Earth. Gogzi estimated it had been at least a week. Needless to say, nobody had tidied or loaded the dishwasher. Gogzi wasn't bothered by the mess, but it made her task a little more difficult.

The smell of the goblin sleeping potion was stronger in the kitchen but she couldn't see it. Closing her eyes, Gogzi allowed the invisible guiding hand of the scent to draw her towards it. She turned round, crouched down and crawled along the floor, sniffing like a dog. Then she had it! A stone pot with a cork stopper was tucked at the back of the bottom cupboard. She grabbed it and pulled out the cork. Inside was the tell-tale slimy purple of a goblin sleeping potion. Gogzi snickered and whispered quietly to herself, 'Now we is see...'

There was beer and cider still unopened in one of the cupboards, and two blocks of the cheese that James, outside, was craving. Gogzi had to look in the freezer for bread; the goblin boy had eaten all the fresh loaf.

Gogzi had just poured a big mug of cider when she heard the hiss at the kitchen door. It looked so like James, but it wasn't him. It said nothing, but it opened its eyes wide and gave a little snarl, spreading its hands and shrugging as if asking Gogzi what she thought she was doing.

"Ah! Hello! Me is Gogzi! Me is visit this best house," Gogzi said pleasantly, suggesting that everything was normal. "You is have best food, here!"

The goblin boy shook his head at Gogzi and raised a finger to his lips as if to say, 'Shh.' Then he waggled it disapprovingly and frowned, pointing at the food and then at himself. From this Gogzi understood him to mean that it all belonged to him.

"Oh is your food, yes?" Gogzi asked, pretending ignorance and innocence. "Well is plenty. Come. We is share."

The little goblin eyed his older fellow suspiciously, but then looked at the impromptu meal. Gogzi had made cheese on toast and the sight and the smell of it was very enticing. The changeling had obviously been eating mainly out of packets and tins for days. He moved slowly over to the kitchen table and slid into one of the chairs. Greedily he grabbed a piece of toast with its delicious, golden, melted topping, and crammed it into his mouth, gobbling it down quickly before reaching out for another.

Gogzi grinned and poured some cider into a mug. The little creature's eyes opened wide. Still staring at Gogzi, he took the mug from her and slurped down the contents. He wasn't the brightest, thought Gogzi. Within the minute, the imposter was slumped over the kitchen table, fast asleep.

Chapter 8

Return

"You did it!" James said, unnecessarily, when he saw the sleeping figure. Gogzi had run to the door to fetch the two waiting outside. James was about to cram a slice of toast into his mouth when Gogzi stopped him and handed him a different piece.

"Is better eat this one. Unless James is want sleep too!" James looked at her and gave a big nod.

"Oh!" he said. "I nearly forgot! There's no potion in this one though, is there?" Gogzi shook her head.

"No. Is best cheese toast me ever is make!" she giggled. "Goblin-boy James is be not clever. Me is mix sleep-sleep potion. He is not notice. Now we is be quick before he is wake!"

James' heart was beating fast. They needed to get the goblins back to their own realm before the potion wore off. He felt in his pocket for the medallion. If he pulled the two parts away from each other, would a door open up in his own kitchen? How would they know? What would be waiting on the other side? In spite of his questions, James drew the medallion out and held it up for Gogzi to see.

"Are you ready?" he asked.

"Me is ready." Gogzi had both arms wrapped tightly round the lookalike James, primed to take him through the portal as soon as it opened. James looked at her for a moment. So much had changed in the last two days. Gogzi had started out as an enemy – a captor. Now that he was about to send her back to her own land forever, he felt a pang of something. Gogzi had helped him – maybe because of some sort of goblin sense of honour. The debt would now be repaid. He would never see her again. James felt for a moment as though he was about to lose a friend. It was Dexter who broke his train of thought.

"Hurry up!" he quacked. "And thanks for all your help. Hope we don't meet again!"

Gogzi laughed and said, "You is welcome, horrid duck-friend!"

Taking a deep breath, James pulled the two parts of the medallion. He had expected some resistance — like a strange force holding them together — but they came apart easily as though there was no magic involved.

For a second, there was silence as the three of them, with their unconscious victim, stood together in the kitchen. Then suddenly there was a rush of dank air and James knew the portal had been opened. He could not see where it was, but Gogzi could.

She lifted the goblin boy and dragged him towards the invisible entrance and then James could just make out the dark swampland stretching into the distance and he could hear the sounds of small creatures. He helped Gogzi bundle the sleeping goblin through. Their plan was nearly complete!

James began to think of his father who would be waking soon as the potion wore off. He wasn't sure how or what he would tell him. With the two goblins nearly through, James started to wave his goodbye to Gogzi. He lifted the medallion again, ready to secure the barrier. Suddenly, to his horror, four pairs of dark green goblin hands reached through the opening, roughly grabbed Gogzi and the sleeping changeling and dragged them back into the goblin realm. In his shock, James clamped the medallion together and sealed them on the other side.

For a moment, both boy and duck looked at each other, mouth and bill respectively open in dismay. Gogzi's plan had worked beautifully. They had captured the goblin changeling and opened the portal to get him to the other side. Now dad could wake up and everything could go back to normal. Except they had delivered Gogzi straight into the hands of the other goblins and they did not look friendly. James knew what they did with their human prisoners. How would they treat a fellow goblin that had betrayed them? James stared at the medallion in his hands. He had sealed the portal. No goblins would be able to come back to steal babies any more. The humans were safe. But...

"I'm sure she'll be fine!" Dexter quacked, reading James' mind. "She's with her own kind and she's clever. She'll know what to do, don't worry."

James bit his lip. Maybe Dexter was right. It was Gogzi's choice and she was definitely a clever little goblin, no matter what Naklog had said. She certainly seemed to be able to look after herself. He nodded slowly but he felt a sick feeling in the pit of his stomach.

"Let's go and see if we can wake up your dad," Dexter continued. James followed him slowly, nibbling on his piece of toasted cheese. His appetite had disappeared, even though he could still feel the gnawing inside that came from not having eaten for two days.

Dad was still unconscious. James called him and shook him, but he grunted and muttered something in his sleep about taking James for a haircut and went back to snoring. Eventually, not able to wait any longer, James went to the kitchen and brought back a bowl of cold water. It was a bit drastic, but he wanted his dad awake.

He tipped the bowl up and the contents splashed over his dad, drenching his face and clothes, and running on to the chair and floor. But it worked. He spluttered and shouted, "Hey!" then sat up, rubbed the water out of his eyes and gawped at James.

"James!" he yelled. "What are you doing? Is this some kind of a practical joke?" Then he looked around himself, confused.

"What's going on? Why am I in this chair? Was I asleep?"

James toyed with the idea of telling his dad everything but it was a long, fantastic story that would need the right time and this wasn't it. Instead, he opted for a simpler version that had some truth in it. He and Dexter had been staying over at a friend's house and when they had returned, Dad had been asleep. Getting worried that he was not waking up, James had used the cold water method. Later he would explain why so many days had passed without his dad knowing.

"Well, did you have to be so extreme?" Dad complained, still dazed and looking down at himself, wondering why he was wearing his work clothes.

"I think I need to get out of these," he muttered, heading upstairs to the bathroom where James could hear him turning on the shower and grumbling to himself.

James sat down on the couch and stared at the floor. He felt awful. He had eaten and he had awoken Dad. Tonight, instead of a cold cave floor, he could sleep in his lovely bed – after changing the sheets, of course! But he was troubled. He could not stop thinking about Gogzi on the other side of the barrier.

Dexter was outside paddling and ducking in the pond. James watched him. It was such a relief to have him back, safe and sound and he had been a good friend, diving in the mud to fetch the medallion. Gogzi had been a good friend too. Without her, they would not have succeeded.

Dexter popped his head up and caught James' eye through the window. They both stared at each other. Then Dexter jumped out of the pond and shook his feathers dry. He waddled in through the back door and into the living room, where James still stood.

"You're going back, aren't you?" he quacked.

"I have to, Dexter," James replied, "You don't..."

"...abandon your friends." They finished the sentence together and James laughed sheepishly. Dexter gave a resigned sigh with a shrug and half a nod.

"It's alright, though. I'm not expecting you to come with me," James went on. "I just want to make sure she's OK."

"Of course I'm coming with," Dexter retorted. "Who will look after you if I'm not there? And anyway – I don't think I could easily explain to Dad what happened to you if you don't come back, never mind put up with his awful jokes all by myself! This time, though, it'll be on our terms and they won't know we're coming!"

James agreed. They took his school backpack and filled it with the items they thought would be useful: the bolt-cutters from his dad's toolbox, a roll of duct tape, the goblin knife James had taken and the head-torch he gave Dad last birthday. Dad used it for when he was cycling in the winter.

It was a bit big for James but he managed to tighten the elasticated straps to make it fit his head. When it was turned on, the light had a powerful, bright beam that was good for being seen by cars – or for lighting up goblin tunnels.

"OK, here goes," he said, taking the medallion from his pocket and pulling the pieces apart. James still could not see where the portal had opened, but he could feel the tell-tale breeze. Dexter quacked, "This way!" and James followed him into the goblin realm, making sure to put the two medallion pieces back together on the other side.

Chapter 9

Prisoner

It was still dark on this side of the portal, but James did not dare turn on the head-torch yet for fear of being detected by the goblins. He was sure they would have taken Gogzi back to the caves where he and Dexter had been held prisoner. If Gogzi was still alive, James would find a way to set her free. Dexter was already getting ready to fly and James was relieved he had come. Without him, he was not sure he would have known where to go.

For miles around, the goblin scenery looked the same: dull marshland punctuated only by the rocky ruins of old dwellings and those small, bare trees. Looking up at Dexter, outlined against the pale moonlit sky, James ran and stumbled and dragged his feet out of the squelchy mud but kept going until they reached the cave entrance again.

No goblins were visible nearby, but James and Dexter were cautious. The duck flapped to the ground and James picked him up. It would be quieter and quicker to carry him. James waited to catch his breath before entering and then silently made his way through the dark passages.

When he turned his head-torch on, he shuddered at the sight of the remains that were glued to the walls, but forced himself to look, in case Gogzi was among them. At one point, his heart leapt at the sight of a young goblin of Gogzi's size hanging near a fork in the tunnels – but it was another poor soul that had obviously fallen foul of the tribe.

The tunnels seemed endless. When they had been running to escape them, they had not needed to look in all the nooks and crannies that sprouted off in different directions. There were forks and bends and dead-ends and so many smaller branches of the tunnels that James had never noticed before. But they searched them all, in case their friend had been stashed away. Slowly the old, familiar sound of goblin revelry reached their ears. Dexter glanced up at James.

"They're celebrating," he quacked quietly. "I hope we're not too late."

James put that thought from his mind and hurried, following the sound. Before long, the goblin shouts and singing led him to a large stone chamber – the goblin hall. It was lit by the flaming orange torches that were protruding from the walls and in the very centre was a huge fire blazing from a pit in the floor. James turned off his head-torch and placed Dexter quietly on the ground. The two of them lurked in the shadows by the stony arch that was the hall entrance.

Goblins of all sizes were gathered in the hall, singing noisily and drinking from cups made of wood and horn. At the top of a flight of stone steps, on a great throne cut straight from the rock at the far end of the hall, sat a small goblin in a crude gold crown, his claw-like feet resting on a large chest. He wore a rough, reddish cloak, and long, greasy hair framed his wrinkled face. James was surprised. If that was the goblin king, he was smaller and older than he had imagined.

At that point, his thoughts were interrupted by an insistent pecking on the shin. Dexter was trying to show him that suspended from the ceiling of the hall, not far from the central fire, was a cage. Inside it, slumped against the bars, was the unmistakable shape of their friend, Gogzi.

James' hand went involuntarily to his mouth and he stifled a cry of dismay. The goblins had been angry with Gogzi's treachery. He was sure they intended to put her cage into the flames once they had tired of parading her for all to see. James could not – he *would* not – let that happen to his friend.

Chapter 10
Suspended

Hidden from the goblin throng, in the shadows by the entrance, James communicated silently with Dexter. It would be tricky, but Dexter nodded as James mimed the plan with his hands and then retrieved the duct tape from his rucksack. After a moment, and with a quiet intake of breath, he gave Dexter a nod, and the bird flew into the hall.

Dexter did not try to avoid detection this time; he quacked as loudly as he could whilst flapping just out of reach of the alarmed goblins whose songs turned into angry shouts. Dexter was almost enjoying himself. He was far too good a flyer to be hit by the hurled cups and bits of goblin bread, but he was achieving his purpose: to make as much commotion as possible and to distract the goblins from James, who by now, had crept unnoticed, up to the King's throne. Before the King had a chance to respond, James had wrapped him tightly with the tape, securing his thin, little arms to his sides.

The King wriggled and began to squeal. The noise caused a couple of nearby goblins to turn, their mouths open in surprise and fury, but by then,

James had already grabbed one of the giant hooks from the wall, slipped the end of it under the tape restraint and had begun to hoist the King into the air like a small, squealing bag of potatoes. The King kicked his tiny legs but James only pulled him higher and swung him over the central pit, where he continued to squeal loudly but stopped wriggling for fear of breaking loose and falling in.

All the goblins in the room gawped in amazement, glancing first at James and then at their King, whilst Dexter still harried them from above. They were stupid with drink and the surprise of the attack, but slowly they began to work out that a human boy was holding the end of the chain that went over a pulley in the hall ceiling and dangled their King over the pit of fire. James did not wait for them to make up their minds about what to do or how loyal they wanted to be to their King.

"Stay right there or I drop him!" he shouted. The goblins seemed to be considering this but James could see some beginning to shuffle towards him, showing their teeth. Holding the chain with his left hand he reached up with his right and switched his head-torch on. They stopped instantly, dazzled by its sudden brightness.

"Quick!" he shouted to Dexter. The duck landed on the King's head and snatched the crown, throwing it on to the ground in front of the largest group of goblins. Instinctively, they all dived towards it, each one wanting to grab it for themselves. At the same time, James kicked hard at the wooden chest, causing it to tip over and smash on the stone steps.

James had guessed right. Gold coins spilled out and cascaded down away from the throne and across the hall. Goblins who had not made it to the crown in time, now rushed towards this new booty and scrabbled over each other for the coins. Dexter, meanwhile, reached down to a large gold ring that the King had looped on his belt. Attached to this was a rusty, metal key that James hoped was the right one. Dexter grabbed it and flew up to the cage, where a now completely alert Gogzi was watching. The duck passed the key to her through the bars.

For a moment, she grappled with it clumsily, stretching her long arms through the bars and struggling to make it turn in the lock. Dexter was afraid she was going to drop it. Then suddenly with a click, the cage was open and like a monkey, Gogzi scrambled up the chain which held the cage, to the pulley at the top and down the other side, joining James by the wall.

With the gold now the centre of several skirmishes, the goblins seemed less interested in their disgraced King, but James worried that they would quickly turn their attention to Gogzi and himself. She seemed to know what to do, however.

Taking the chain from him, she hooked their end of it to an iron bar that jutted out of the cave wall. This meant that the King was still dangling precariously over the fire without James having to hold on. He was safely clear of the heat from the reaching flames, but still he squealed and called to the goblins to help him. Grabbing the other chain that had held her cage, Gogzi shoved it into James' hand and cried, "Here! Is not let go!" And with that, she kicked off against the wall, holding tight to James with both hands, and the pair of them swung like pirates from the mast of a tall ship, making a graceful arc around the giant hall and landing neatly just before the cave entrance.

James let out a laugh, half triumph and half relief, as the three of them pelted down the corridor, leaving the goblins to either fight over the gold or to release their King.

"Gold is be keep goblins for little time," Gogzi panted, "Not big time.

James and horrid duck is be hurry-hurry."

Neither James nor Dexter needed telling. They were both wide-eyed with excitement and fear as they hurtled through the tunnels.

Chapter 11

Fartlebeast

They had not yet seen the light of the exit when a familiar smell reached James' nostrils and they stumbled into a chamber where they found the fartlebeast. She rumbled miserably and peered at them over the top of a rough, leather muzzle which covered her snout. One of her back legs was clamped with an iron ring and held fast by a chain bolted to the wall.

James could see that in her struggles she had worn away the fur and skin round the ring and left a nasty red wound. Marks across her flanks showed where the goblins had beaten her. She had obviously been left there in disgrace for running off with the glued goblin. Piles of dung covered the floor, showing that she had been tied up for some time and James could see no sign of food or water for her. Cowering beneath the fartlebeast, and making sad little whimpering snuffles, was her baby.

Dexter quacked angrily at the evidence of the goblins' cruelty. Silently, James agreed that they could not leave her there, tied up like this.

Quickly, he took off his backpack and removed the bolt-cutters. Both he and Gogzi had to lean on them with all their might, but eventually, with a loud 'ping', they cut through the metal ring that held the beast's leg. Dexter, meanwhile, using his bill, undid the straps of the muzzle and freed the mother beast from the harsh leather. She gave a loud snort and covered him in sticky mucus.

"Thanks!" he quacked, shaking off the fartlebeast snot. In spite of the danger they were in, James laughed quietly. The fartlebeast turned to him and Gogzi and licked both their faces with a tongue that felt like wet sandpaper.

"Ew!" James said and wiped his face with his sleeve. He smiled, though, and bent down to give a friendly scratch to the baby fartlebeast that was now nibbling and tugging at his trainer laces. Gogzi spat in exaggerated disgust but gave the mum a friendly ruffle of the fur on her head.

"Stinky beast is need go now!" she whispered, giving her a little push. However, the animal did not move but stood looking at her expectantly, and when Gogzi shrugged and began to pull the others away, the great creature followed her like an obedient pet dog.

"Listen!" Dexter quacked as they began to move off. They paused, straining their ears. Distant goblin shouts could be heard, but the squeals of the dangling King had stopped. The goblins had either rescued their leader or had allowed him to be dropped into the fire. James shivered at the thought. He wasn't sure if the goblins would commit regicide, but either way, the chances were that they would be coming after the escaped prisoners soon enough. Now that the excitement of the rescue had begun to wane, James began to notice how exhausted he was.

"I don't know if I can run much further!" he shouted, as they jogged from the dark tunnel into the breaking dawn of the goblin day. "This stuff is really hard to run in!" he continued, looking down at the boggy surface that was slowing him down and soaking his shoes.

"Yes. James is be too tired!" Gogzi nodded. "But me is have plan!"

"Another plan!" Dexter quacked. "What a surprise!" Secretly he was grateful. Lately, Gogzi's plans had been rather successful.

"James is watch Gogzi now. Is copy." As she ran, she scooped up the baby fartlebeast and leaped nimbly from the soggy marsh on to the mother's back. James took no time to follow suit, though his attempt involved lots more scrabbling and slipping. Eventually, he was straddled over the wide flanks of the great beast. Dexter flew down to settle between him and Gogzi, who was astride the beast's neck, the baby held firmly in front. Gogzi leaned forward and spoke into the mother's ear, and James had to grasp hold of the rough fur to stop himself being thrown off as she accelerated forwards.

It seemed that the fartlebeast was as pleased as they were to be free and she showed this by bounding with surprising speed away from the goblin cave. Generations of fartlebeasts had lived and thrived in these desolate marshlands and she was beautifully adapted to galloping across the boggy ground, her broad feet barely sinking in to the mud as she ran.

Finally, when Gogzi felt they had put sufficient distance between themselves and their pursuers, she leaned forward again, spoke to the fartlebeast and they ground to a halt near the ruin by the lake.

"Is time," Gogzi said briefly.

Chapter 12

Home

James slid stiffly from his position and landed, feet in the mud, with a splash. Dexter stood and gave his wings a flapping stretch before joining him on the soggy ground.

"James is need go. Is close portal," Gogzi said, looking down from the neck of the beast who was huffing and blowing jets of vapour out of her nostrils.

James stared up at the little goblin. It was difficult to know what to say. Awkwardly, he leant towards her and held out his hand in a rather overly-formal gesture. She stared at it for a moment, not knowing the human handshake ritual and then stretched down and gave it a kind of sideways 'high-five', still gripping the baby fartlebeast with the other hand. James smiled and looked down. Neither of them wanted to make the final goodbye and they were each silent waiting for the other to speak.

The sombre moment was shattered by a loud and exceptionally long ripping noise from the rear end of the fartlebeast and they both burst into laughter as she dumped a huge pile of dung on the ground. Dexter waddled out of the way in disgust. The fartlebeast continued to nibble innocently at the swamp weed.

"Phew!" James said, trying but failing to wave the smell away with his hand. "Great timing!" Then he turned back to Gogzi. "Will you be OK? Will they find you? What will you do?"

"Me is be OK," she replied, patting the beast on the shoulder. "Gogzi is best rider. This land is be Gogzi home. Me is know everywhere." She gave a little wave of her upturned hand across the horizon as if they needed to know where she meant. Then she turned back to two of them.

"Goodbye human James! Goodbye horrid duck-friend!" Without

further hesitation, she said, 'Come, Stinky!" to the fartlebeast, who snorted in response and took off. The boy and the duck were left to watch their friend gallop towards the horizon, astride the great animal, clutching the baby with one hand and holding tightly to its fur with the other. They heard her laugh, bounding away across the goblin marshland, the wind loosening her plait so that her red hair broke free and streamed out magnificently behind her as she rode.

***

James stared at the two intertwined trees of the medallion which he held in his hand. He had removed the goblin hair string and now the gold shone with an alarming brightness. When they had returned, Dad had fully woken up but had refused to believe James' cover story of staying with friends and coming home to find him fast asleep. James had ended up telling him the whole thing.

To James' surprise, instead of Dad being cross and disbelieving, he had nodded thoughtfully. Apparently, he had not been completely fooled by the goblin James. The changeling's behaviour was just too different and he had started to get worried, watching the goblin boy and asking him all sorts of questions that he couldn't answer. Eventually, he had made an appointment with the child psychologist. That had frightened the changeling and caused it to spike Dad's drink and send him to sleep.

"I know it's mad, but it sort of fits and it explains a lot of the weird things that have been happening," he said to James. "And there's that..." pointing to the metallic object in James' hands. "What are you going to do with it?"

"I need to hide it. But it has to be safe and the two parts must stay together or the portal will open again."

"I'll do it," Dexter quacked. "...What?" he said to their mute response. "I know where it has to go." Without waiting for further questions or discussion, Dexter took the medallion in his bill and turned to go.

"Wait!" James cried. "What do you mean? Where?"

The three of them stared at each other without speaking. Dad looked confused but then James nodded.

"Ah. OK," he said. "Be careful!"

When Dexter arrived, Naklog, looking like a loose accumulation of old clothes, was outside her hut, poking at something in the water with a long stick. She stepped back when she saw the duck and moved surprisingly quickly for the door.

"No more!" she shouted, flapping her hands in irritation. "I've done everything I'm going to do. Now go away! Leave me..." But she stopped mid-protest and froze in the doorway when she caught the glint of the goblin gold held in Dexter's bill. He dropped it at her feet and she backed off as though it were a scorpion.

"It's OK," he quacked. "Take it. Use it one last time to go home to your daughter. The Goblin King is no longer a threat. If he is still alive, he has other problems to deal with."

She fixed a scowl at Dexter, but moved to the medallion, grabbing it and clutching it close to her chest.

"Why?" she managed to hiss. "Why do you trust me with this?"

"I don't trust you" he replied. "I trust your love for Nuin. You will keep the medallion safe and hidden to protect her. If you use it in Goblin Earth, the goblins will know and will find you. If you let it fall into the wrong hands and the goblins come back to our land, *we* will know and *we* will find you!"

Naklog seemed to understand Dexter's implied threat, because she nodded. Then she ran inside and he could see her gathering some of her pathetic belongings together in sheet. Clutching this makeshift bundle under her arm, Naklog pulled apart the medallion and without further ceremony, stepped from this world and back into her own.

Acknowledgements

Many thanks to all the friends and family who read the various versions of this book and gave critique on cover design and illustrations. A special thanks to the children in Year 6 who first knew about Dexter, read the draft and gave me useful feedback.

ABOUT THE AUTHOR

J A Bowler

J A Bowler originates in Zimbabwe but now lives in Warwickshire and often draws on the local environment in story settings. Having taught primary aged children for the best part of three decades, the author is now a freelance writer and artist who also sometimes plays in bands on saxophones and bass guitar.

You can connect with me on:

Author site: https://jabowler.wordpress.com

Twitter: https://twitter.com/JBowler_author

Email: julietbowler@outlook.com

Also by J A Bowler

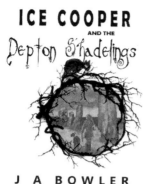

ICE COOPER AND THE Depton Shadelings

J A BOWLER

Ice Cooper and the Depton Shadelings is a supernatural eco-thriller for 9-13 year olds.

Ice Cooper is new to Depton, and as if starting again wasn't hard enough, now she's seeing the strange creatures from her dreams and her dad is lying to her. Why is her mother not answering the phone? And then there are the earthquakes.

Springtail

Printed in Poland
by Amazon Fulfillment
Poland Sp. z o.o., Wrocław